Only Cows Allowed!

by Lynn Plourde

illustrated by Rebecca Harrison Reed

Down East

Story copyright © 2011 by Lynn Plourde. Illustrations © 2011 by Rebecca Harrison Reed.
ISBN: 978-0-89272-790-2
Designed by Lynda Chilton
Printed in Singapore
5   4   3   2

Library of Congress Cataloging-in-Publication Data
Plourde, Lynn.
    Only cows allowed! / by Lynn Plourde ; illustrated by Rebecca Harrison Reed.
        p. cm.
    Summary: The cows try to keep the other animals out of a just-built barn at a New
England farm, insisting that they are the only animals allowed.
    ISBN 978-0-89272-790-2 (hardcover : alk. paper)
    [1. Domestic animals–Fiction. 2. Farm life–New England–Fiction. 3. New England–Fiction.
4. Humorous stories.]   I. Reed, Rebecca, ill. II. Title.
    PZ7.P724On 2011
    [E]–dc22
                                                            2008051824

www.downeast.com
Distributed to the trade by National Book Network

In memory of my mémère,
Catherine Jacques Plourde,
who, unlike the cows, lived by the creed
"ALL welcome!"—LP

For my new nephew and nieces,
Ian, Rowan, and Emma-Graye—RHR

On a new New England farm, with a first-time farmer who loved housecats but hadn't a clue about farm animals— the cows arrived.

They *loved* their new barn and saw no reason why they shouldn't keep it all to themselves.

"ONLY COWS ALLOWED!" the sign said.
And the cows meant it.

The first night was relatively uneventful, with only a couple of cows jumping over the moon.

But early the next morning, there was a *peck-peck-peck* at the barn door.

Hens! The hens had arrived!

"ONLY COWS ALLOWED!" the hens squawked when they saw the cows' sign. "That's ridiculous. We have a right to live here, too."

But the cows wouldn't mooo-ve.

"How do you know we're not really cows in chicken disguises?" asked the hens.

The cows answered, "Milk! You're not cows 'cause you don't give milk."

The hens huddled, hatched a plan, and cackled, "Our milk is coming! Our milk is coming! Quick, get some buckets ready!"

The cows looked skeptical as the hens settled onto the buckets.

Not a single splash—only *plunk-plunk-plunk* as the hens laid egg after egg after egg.

Just then the farmer stepped into the barn and shouted, "What a farmer I am! I've got eggs already!"

He gave the hens a little peck to show his gratitude. "Now if only the cows would give milk," he sighed.

After he left, the hens smugly said, "Gee, that farmer does like eggs. Guess we can stay. Hope he doesn't kick you cows out."

Early the next morning, there was a *clunk-clunk-clunk* at the barn door.

Horses! The horses had arrived!

"ONLY COWS ALLOWED!" the horses neighed when they saw the cows' sign. "That's ridiculous. We have a right to live here, too."

But the cows wouldn't moooooo-ve.

"How do you know we're not really cows in horse disguises?" asked the horses.

The cows answered, "Moo! You're not cows 'cause you don't say *moo*."

The horses corralled themselves, came up with a whinny-ing plan, and said, "Oh, we were just horsing around. We know how to make that sound. Just listen."

The horses pressed their lips together, then opened their mouths wide and . . .

"MEOW! MEOW! MEOW!"

Just then the farmer arrived with an armful of cats. "They don't want to be *house* cats anymore. They want to be *barn* cats. Isn't that cute?"

When the farmer spied the horses, he yelled, "Giddee-up! *Real* farmers go for rides."

"Now if only the cows would moo," he sighed.

When the horses galloped back, they smugly said, "Gee, that farmer *does* like horseback-ward riding. Guess we can stay. Hope he doesn't kick you cows out."

Early the next morning, there was a *honk-honk-honk* at the barn door. A bus! A bus had arrived—filled with pigs, sheep, goats, and geese!

"ONLY COWS ALLOWED!" the pigs, sheep, goats, and geese grunted, baa-ed, maa-ed, and honked when they saw the cows' sign. "That's ridiculous. We have a right to live here, too."

But the cows wouldn't moooooooooo-ve.

"How do you know we're not really cows in pigs, sheep, goats, and geese disguises?"

The cows answered, "Calves! You're not cows 'cause you can't have calves."

The pigs, sheep, goats, and geese answered, "After that bumpy bus ride, we're about to have *something*."

The cows could see they were not kidding, and let them inside, just in the nick of time.

The farmer came to check on all the commotion. When he saw the newborn animals, he shouted, "Yippee-yahoo! Not only am I a *real* farmer, but also a *real* father, too, with all these babies. This calls for a celebration!"

When the farmer returned with a cake, confetti, and party hats, the cows wouldn't mooooooooooo-ve. They knew he wasn't a cow in a farmer disguise because . . .

he didn't chew a cud.

Just then the farmer reached into his pocket, pulled out bunches of bubblegum, and everyone started to chew—not cuds—but *gum*.

At last, the cows surrendered . . .
sighed . . .
mooooooooooooooooo-ved aside . . .
and tried to be good sports at the party.

They did a little line-dancing and hoola-hooping.
But the cows' hearts just weren't in it.

As the all-night party continued, they tiptoed out of the barn, grabbed their sign, and headed into the darkness.

No one even missed them.

"ONLY COWS ALLOWED!" the sign said.
And the cows meant it.